Here's what kids and grown-ups have to say about the Magic Tree House® books:

"Oh, man . . . the Magic Tree House series
is really exciting!"
—Christina

"I like the Magic Tree House series. I stay up
all night reading them. Even on school nights!"
—Peter

"Jack and Annie have opened a door to a world
of literacy that I know will continue throughout
the lives of my students."
—Deborah H.

"As a librarian, I have seen many happy young
readers coming into the library to check out
the next Magic Tree House book in the series."
—Lynne H.

Magic Tree House®

For a list of Magic Tree House® Merlin Missions and other Magic Tree House® titles, visit MagicTreeHouse.com.

MAGIC TREE HOUSE®

#34 LATE LUNCH WITH LLAMAS

BY MARY POPE OSBORNE

ILLUSTRATIONS BY AG FORD

A STEPPING STONE BOOK™

Random House 🏠 New York

To Henry and Rex Corbett

Text copyright © 2020 by Mary Pope Osborne
Cover art and interior illustrations copyright © 2020 by AG Ford

Visit us on the Web!
rhcbooks.com
MagicTreeHouse.com

Educators and librarians, for a variety of teaching tools, visit us at
RHTeachersLibrarians.com

Library of Congress Cataloging-in-Publication Data is available upon request.
ISBN 978-0-525-64840-6 (trade) — ISBN 978-0-525-64841-3 (lib. bdg.) —
ISBN 978-0-525-64842-0 (ebook) — ISBN 978-0-525-64843-7 (pbk.)

Printed in the United States of America

10 9 8 7 6 5 4 3 2 1

This book has been officially leveled by using the F&P Text Level Gradient™
Leveling System.

CONTENTS

PROLOGUE

One summer day in Frog Creek, Pennsylvania, a mysterious tree house appeared in the woods. It was filled with books. A boy named Jack and his sister, Annie, found the tree house and soon discovered that it was magic. They could go to any time and place in history just by pointing to a picture in one of the books. While they were gone, no time at all passed back in Frog Creek.

Jack and Annie eventually found out that the tree house belonged to Morgan le Fay, a magical librarian from the legendary realm of Camelot.

1

Since then, they have traveled on many adventures in the magic tree house and completed many missions for Morgan.

On their last four adventures, Jack and Annie learned great wisdom from heroes of the past.

Morgan is now sending them on four more quests. On these journeys, they must save different creatures in the mysterious world of nature.

1

NOT SO SIMPLE

The late-morning air smelled of honeysuckle. Wind chimes jingled in the summer breeze. Jack sat on the front porch. He was reading a book about whales.

The screen door opened. "Hey," said Jack's sister, Annie.

"Hey," said Jack.

"Guess what? We're going on a picnic at the lake with Mom and Dad," said Annie.

"Great, I'm starving," said Jack. He didn't look up from his book.

"Me too. We're having tomato sandwiches and potato salad," said Annie.

"Cool," said Jack.

"*Yikes*, look!" said Annie. "A giant bird!"

"Funny." Jack kept reading.

"Seriously! Super-big!" shouted Annie. "Look! Look!"

Jack was sure Annie was kidding. But he couldn't help himself. He looked up at the sky.

"Whoa!" he said.

An enormous black-and-white bird was circling above the house. It had a wingspan of at least ten feet!

"I don't believe it!" cried Jack. He jumped up from his chair. "It's a condor!"

"What's that?" asked Annie.

"The world's biggest vulture!" said Jack. "Condors survive by eating mostly dead animals. Sometimes they hunt small living ones."

"Oh, that's sad!" said Annie.

"No. It's nature," said Jack. "Condors are amazing. But they don't live in Pennsylvania! How did it get here?"

The condor flapped its wings and rose higher into the sky. It curved and glided toward the Frog Creek woods.

"It's a sign!" said Annie.

"Come on!" said Jack. He grabbed his backpack.

"Mom! Dad! We're going to the woods," Annie called through the screen door.

"We'll be back in time for the picnic!" yelled Jack.

He and Annie hurried off the porch. They crossed their yard and ran down the sidewalk.

"There it is," said Annie, pointing.

The condor was soaring above the trees. It vanished behind the treetops.

"Go! Go!" yelled Jack.

Jack and Annie ran down their sidewalk and dashed into the Frog Creek woods. Sunlight streamed between the trees. Jack and Annie ran through shadows and light until they came to the tallest oak.

In the branches at the top of the oak was the magic tree house.

"Yay!" said Annie.

"Where's the condor?" asked Jack.

"Maybe we can see it from up there!" said Annie. She and Jack scrambled up the rope ladder and into the tree house.

A book lay on the floor in a pool of sunlight.

Jack picked it up. On the cover was a photo of tree-covered mountains rising above white clouds.

"Wow, beautiful," said Annie. She read the title of the book:

Travel Guide: The Andes Mountains of Peru

"Andes Mountains?" said Jack. "I've always wanted to go there."

"Me too," said Annie. "Uncle Josh went there, remember? To Machu Picchu!" She opened the cover of the travel guide. A folded piece of parchment fell to the floor.

Annie picked it up. "A note from Morgan," she said. She unfolded the note and read aloud:

High on Old Mountain
Is a creature to save.
Bring back the small one.
Find the secret of brave.

When faced with great danger,
Old legends will help you.
Words from your book
Will give you a clue.

Annie looked up. "Okay," she said. "Ready?"

"Hold on," said Jack. "Is that all she wrote?"

"Yep," said Annie. "We go to Old Mountain. We save the small one. Old legends will help us. Short and simple."

"Not so simple," said Jack. "What *is* the small one? Plus, there are thousands of words in this book. How do we find the right clues? And what the heck is the 'secret of brave'?"

Annie sighed. "Let's answer one question at a time. We can't solve a problem until we know what it is."

"You sound like Mom," said Jack. "Okay. Ready to go?"

"Ready for anything!" said Annie.

Jack pointed at the mountains on the cover of the travel guide.

"I wish we could go to the Andes Mountains in Peru!" he said.

The wind started to blow.

The tree house started to spin.

It spun faster and faster.

Then everything was still.

Absolutely still.

2

Young Mountain

Birdsong filled a mountain forest. The air smelled of cedar, pine, and woodsmoke.

"Oh, wow!" said Annie. "I love our clothes!"

She and Jack both wore bright red wool ponchos, brown cotton pants and shirts, leather sandals, and green knit caps with earflaps and purple tassels.

"Colorful," said Jack.

"And warm!" said Annie.

Their ponchos were heavy and hung down to their knees. Jack's backpack had turned into a woven cloth bag. It hung by a strap across his chest.

Annie and Jack looked out the window.

"Oh, wow," said Annie. "It's really pretty here."

The tree house had landed in a tall pine tree in a forest of pines, cedars, and trees with huge hanging pods. Mountains rose on the horizon. Feathery clouds floated below their peaks.

"The Andes Mountains," said Jack. He opened their travel guide to the first page. He read aloud:

The Andes are the longest mountain range in the world. They run from the top to the tip of South America, a distance of 4,350 miles. High in the Andes of Peru, tourists hike through cloud forests and mountain meadows.

"*Cloud forests* and *mountain meadows*," repeated Annie. "That sounds beautiful."

11

Jack turned the pages. He stopped at a photo of men and women dressed in red ponchos and hats. The caption said:

Wool ponchos have been worn by natives of the Andes for many centuries.

"Many centuries?" said Jack. "So, what century is this?"

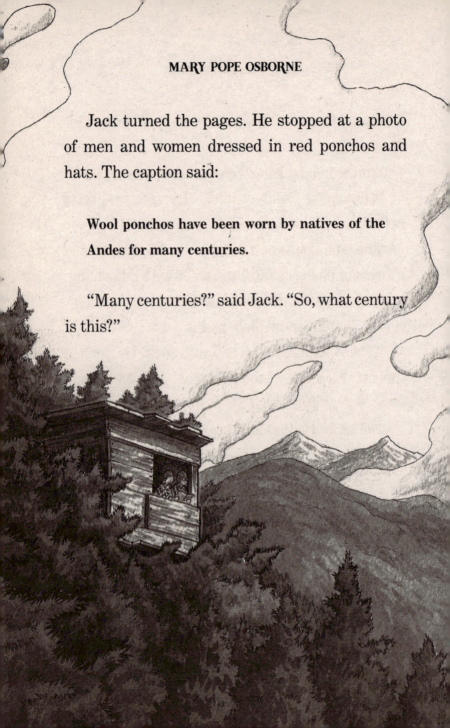

"I don't know, but I have a feeling we came to a time long ago," said Annie.

"Me too," said Jack. "But I'm not sure why I feel that way."

"Whoa, what's *that* sound?" said Annie.

"What sound?" said Jack.

"Music! Hear it?" said Annie.

Jack listened carefully. Sweet, airy music floated through the cloud forest.

"It's a flute, I think," Jack said.

"Let's check it out," said Annie.

Jack put the travel guide into his bag. He followed Annie down the rope ladder. They stepped together into the tangled brush.

The cloud forest buzzed with insect sounds. Hummingbirds and butterflies flitted among red and purple flowers. A pale green frog leapt over a tree root.

"The flute music is coming from over there," said Annie. Following the sound, Jack and Annie walked between the trees. They climbed over rocks and roots. They pushed through towering ferns.

Soon they came to a clearing. They saw an elderly couple sitting outside a small hut.

"We found the music," said Annie.

"Shh," Jack whispered. "Don't let them hear you."

The old man was sitting on the grass, playing a

wooden flute. The woman was lifting potatoes out of a red-hot fire pit.

"This feels like a long time ago, doesn't it?" whispered Annie.

"Yeah," breathed Jack. "Look, llamas!"

"Oh, wow," whispered Annie.

In a small meadow behind the hut, several llamas were quietly grazing. They had woolly white coats, long necks, and camel-like faces. Their curved ears were shaped like bananas.

"They're so cute," whispered Annie.

Jack had to agree. The llamas *were* cute.

"I love llamas," whispered Annie.

"Who doesn't?" said Jack.

"No, I *really* love them," whispered Annie.

"Why do people keep llamas?" Jack wondered out loud.

"Look it up," said Annie.

Jack pulled the Andes travel guide from his bag and searched in the index for *llamas*. When

15

he found the right page, he and Annie read silently together:

Llamas are the most important animal in the Andes. For centuries, they've provided mountain people with wool and carried their things. The Incas once believed llamas were protected by a star constellation shaped like a mother and a baby llama. Inca legend says that in early times, llamas could talk.

"Cool! Talking llamas!" Annie said with a laugh.

The old man and woman looked over at Jack and Annie. The man put down his flute. He and the woman stood up.

"Hello! We come in peace!" Annie called. Smiling, she headed over to the couple.

Oh, brother, thought Jack, following her. How would they explain who they were?

"I'm Annie! And this is my brother, Jack," said Annie. "We stopped to listen to your beautiful music."

The couple smiled and nodded. They seemed shy but friendly.

"You have beautiful llamas, too," said Annie. "Don't they, Jack?"

"Um, yeah . . . we like llamas . . . a lot," said Jack.

"Where do you come from, Jack and Annie?" the man asked.

"We're visiting Peru from Frog Creek, Pennsylvania," said Annie.

The couple looked puzzled.

"Right now we're just hiking," Jack said quickly. "Um, walking."

"You came from the valley and climbed up Young Mountain?" asked the man.

Jack nodded. "Uh, yes," he said. "That's what we did."

"What a long way," the woman said. Her dark eyes were kind. "Would you like something to eat?"

Jack couldn't resist. "Yes, thank you," he said.

The woman reached for two potatoes wrapped in leaves near the fire pit. "These are—"

Before she could finish, cries came from the forest. "Grandmother! Grandfather!" someone howled.

"Topa!" said the old man.

A small barefoot boy ran into the meadow. He looked much younger than Jack and Annie. As

18

he ran toward his grandparents, he waved his arms.

"They took her away!" he cried. "They took Cria away!"

"Who took her?" said his grandmother.

"Two men!" Topa cried. "They had spears and helmets with feathers!"

Spears? Helmets with feathers? We definitely came to a time long ago, Jack thought.

"Royal guards," the grandfather said.

The old woman gasped and shook her head. "Oh, no!" she said. She hugged her grandson. "Are you all right?"

"Yes! But they took Cria away!" the boy cried again. "Near the bridge! That's where they stole her from me!"

"Who is Cria?" said Jack. "Is she your little sister?"

"No!" wailed Topa, raising his head. "Not my little sister! My baby *llama!*"

3

That Bridge?

"They stole your baby llama?" said Annie.

"Yes!" cried Topa. "She belongs to me!"

"Cria is an orphan, and so is Topa," said the old man. "Now Cria is Topa's whole world. He takes great care of her."

"I tried to fight them," said Topa. "But they laughed at me. They took her across the bridge. It was so foggy I couldn't see them. I heard them laughing. I heard her crying. I heard her little bell ringing."

"Why did they steal her?" asked Annie.

Topa wiped his eyes. "One man said, 'Grab her! Her coat shines like silver! There are none like her anywhere in the Secret City,'" said Topa.

"The Secret City!" said Topa's grandmother with dismay.

"The Secret City?" Jack repeated. "What's that?"

"It's near the top of Old Mountain," said Topa's grandfather. "There's no hope if they take the small one up there."

Topa let out a wail. He buried his head against his grandmother and shook with sobs.

"Oh, I am sorry, Topa. I am so sorry," the old woman said, rocking him.

"The small one!" Annie said to Jack. *"Old Mountain!"* They're both in our rhyme."

"I know," said Jack. He remembered:

High on Old Mountain
Is a creature to save.

21

Bring back the small one.
Find the secret of brave.

"This is our mission! We have to save her!" Annie said.

Overhearing Annie, Topa whirled around. "You will help?" he said through his tears. "You will find Cria and bring her back home?"

"We will try," said Annie.

"No. You cannot," the old man said sharply. "You are not allowed in the Secret City. None of us are."

"No more talk of this," said the old woman. "Jack and Annie climbed up from the valley, Topa. They must return home now. Here." She handed Jack two baked potatoes wrapped in leaves. "Take these for your journey."

"Oh . . . okay . . . thank you," said Jack. He put the warm potatoes into his bag.

"Grandmother, can I show them the short way back to the valley?" asked Topa, wiping his tears.

"Yes," said the old woman, nodding. "Show them the path. Then come straight home." She looked at Jack and Annie. "After Topa points out the way, you must send him back to us."

"Don't worry," said Jack. "We will."

"Follow me, Jack and Annie," said Topa. The small barefoot boy started out of the meadow.

"Thank you for the potatoes," Jack said to the old couple. Then he and Annie hurried to catch up with Topa.

When they were out of sight of his grandparents, Topa grabbed Annie's hand.

"You're not really going home now, are you?" he asked. "First you'll find Cria in the Secret City?"

"Yes, of course. We'll do our best," said Annie.

23

"Wait," said Jack. "We don't know anything about this Secret City. What is it?"

"I do not know," said Topa. "It's a secret. Why—are you afraid?"

"No, I'm not afraid," said Jack. "How do we get there?"

"Come, I will take you to the rope bridge," said Topa.

Jack and Annie followed the boy between the pines and cedars. Topa led them through high ferns and bushes, and under more trees with giant hanging pods.

"Topa, what do we do after we cross the bridge?" Annie asked. "Is there a path?"

"Yes, on the other side is the Old Trail," said Topa. "They took Cria that way. But you shouldn't follow them. They might see you. There is another way to the Secret City."

"What is it?" said Jack.

"After you cross the bridge, climb through the

brush up to the high ridge," said Topa. "I have heard Grandfather say it's faster than the Old Trail. But watch out for snakes."

"Snakes?" said Jack. "Did you say *snakes*?"

Topa stopped and looked back at them. "Yes. Why—are you afraid of snakes?"

"No, I'm good. Keep going," said Jack.

Topa led them through the brush to the misty edge of Young Mountain. Jack heard the distant roar of a rushing river. Across the way he could barely see the peak of Old Mountain. It was partially hidden by clouds.

"There! That's the rope bridge!" said Topa.

A sagging footbridge stretched over the gap between the two mountains. The bridge swayed in the breeze. It seemed to be made entirely of rope, even its railings.

"*That's* the bridge?" said Jack. "Seriously?"

"Yes," said Topa.

"Yikes," said Annie.

"Don't worry; I'll look in the guide," Jack said. "There has to be a different way to cross."

"No, there is not," said Topa. "This is the *only* way from Young Mountain to Old Mountain."

"But this bridge looks really unsafe," Jack said.

"The royal guards crossed it," said Topa. "And Cria did, too. Are you afraid to cross?"

"No, I'm not," said Jack, annoyed.

"Actually, Jack is afraid," Annie said. "But he's—"

"Annie! Actually, I'm *not* afraid," said Jack.

"Oh. Okay. I just—" started Annie.

"Forget it," said Jack. "I've got this. Come on! Let's cross the bridge!"

4

Mountain Sickness

"Thank you, Jack and Annie!" said Topa. "After we cross, I will lead you through the forest to the Secret City!"

"No, Topa," said Annie. "I'm sorry, but you can't come with us. We promised your grandparents that we would send you home."

"But you need me to help you find Cria!" Topa cried. "I am old enough! I am not afraid!"

"We know you're very brave, Topa," said Annie. "And that's why you have to go back and take care of your grandparents. They need you."

Topa started to protest. There were tears in his eyes.

"If you don't go home, we won't go to the Secret City," said Annie. "We have to keep our promise."

The small boy sighed. "All right. You go."

"We'll see you later," Annie said kindly. "And we'll bring Cria back."

"Be very careful," said Topa. "If the guards see you—"

"I know, we've got this," said Jack. "Come on, Annie. Let's just go."

Jack stepped onto the bridge. As soon as he did, it swung from side to side.

"Whoa!" Jack said.

"Careful," said Annie.

"I'm okay," said Jack. He gripped the rope railings with both hands.

He carefully placed one foot in front of the other. When he looked down, he saw a rushing river far below. Foamy water flowed through a narrow gap between steep mountainsides.

Jack stopped. The sight made him dizzy.

"Don't look down!" Annie called. "I'm right behind you."

"Good plan," Jack whispered. He looked up and took a deep breath.

Jack inched his hands along the rope railings. Walking carefully, step by step, he stared through the mist at Old Mountain. His heart was pounding.

"So far, so good!" Annie called.

"Sort of . . . pretty much . . . ," Jack whispered.

The bridge was swaying. He could hear the roar of the river below. But he kept going until he reached the end and stepped onto Old Mountain.

Annie stepped off the bridge a moment later.

"We made it," breathed Jack.

"Good luck!" Topa shouted. The small boy

waved from the other end of the bridge. Then he turned and disappeared between the trees.

Jack pointed to a stone path that led away from the bridge. "That must be the trail the guards took," he said.

"Right," said Annie. "But Topa said we shouldn't go that way. We should go through the forest up to the Secret City."

"Hold on. I need to check something first," Jack said. He pulled out their Andes travel guide and looked in the index for *snakes*. He turned to the right page and read aloud:

Peru has 200 species of snakes. Three types found in Andean cloud forests are shown here.

Below was the photo of a red snake with black and yellow bands. The caption said *harmless milk snake.*

Another photo showed a dark snake with a pale belly. The caption said *very rare fishing snake.*

A third showed a black-and-green snake. The label said *highly venomous pit viper.*

"Whoa," said Jack.

"What does *venomous* mean?" said Annie.

"It means that if it bites you, you could die," said Jack. He closed the book. "Okay, I have a question."

"What?" said Annie.

"Why does Morgan want us to work so hard just to save one little llama?" said Jack. "It doesn't make sense."

Annie thought for a moment. Then she said, "Yes, it does. Sometimes small things are huge things. To Topa, his baby llama is as big as the whole world."

"Okay. I get that," said Jack, nodding. "Let's go on. But keep an eye out for snakes. Especially black-and-green ones."

Jack and Annie started up through the jungle-like forest that led to the Secret City.

As they climbed through brush and weeds, Jack looked around for snakes. Struggling through tangles of vines, brambles, and prickly shrubs, he was still on alert.

"OW!" Annie shrieked.

Jack jumped. "What? A snake?" he cried.

"No! Thorns!" said Annie. "I got scratched!"

"That's all?" said Jack. "You didn't have to make such a big deal about it."

"I didn't," said Annie. "I just said 'Ow.'"

"Whatever," said Jack. "Maybe we should have taken the Old Trail. It probably doesn't have thorns—or snakes."

"Too late now," said Annie. "Just keep going."

Jack and Annie kept climbing. As they made their way up the mountain, Jack felt less alert. He started feeling faint and short of breath.

Annie stopped. "Something's . . . wrong . . . ," she said, huffing and puffing.

"Yeah . . . ," murmured Jack. "Let's take a break. . . ." He stopped near a pile of rocks.

"Good . . . idea," said Annie.

Gasping for breath, they both sank to the ground.

Jack felt like he might throw up. "Maybe . . . we're getting mountain sickness," he said.

"What's that?" said Annie.

"I don't know exactly . . . but I've heard of it," said Jack. He pulled out their travel guide. He looked up *mountain sickness.*

"It's here," Jack said. He read aloud:

Mountain Sickness: People breathe oxygen to live. The higher you climb, the less oxygen there is. If you go up the Andes too quickly, you can feel sick and have trouble catching your breath. Climb slowly to give your body time to get used to less oxygen. Drink lots of water.

"We don't have water," said Annie, panting. "But . . . but we can go slower."

"Right . . . slower . . . ," said Jack.

"AHH!" Annie shrieked, leaping up.

"What! WHAT?" Jack yelled, leaping with her.

"Snakes!" she cried.

5

Go Slow Fast!

A black-and-green snake was sliding out from the underbrush. Then Jack saw another!

"Pit vipers!" he yelled, springing up from the ground. *"Venomous!"*

The two pit vipers slithered away between the rocks.

"Go! Go!" Jack shouted to Annie.

"Go *slow*!" she yelled, hurrying after him.

"Go slow *fast*!" cried Jack.

They scrambled up the mountain slope.

The snake scare gave them a burst of energy.

But after a while, they grew tired and short of breath again.

"I . . . I need to . . . stop . . . ," said Annie, panting.

"Up ahead . . . short way . . . ," Jack gasped. "A clearing . . . keep going."

Jack and Annie pushed themselves harder, climbing through brush and tall plants, until they came to an open area.

"Stop . . . here. . . ." Jack could barely get the words out.

Just below the misty mountaintop, the forest had been cleared. A series of low stone walls had been built on the slope. Between the walls were narrow, flat fields.

"What are these walls?" said Annie, still breathless.

"I think they're called terraces," said Jack. "The walls keep rocks and mud from sliding down mountains."

"Looks like . . . a stairway for giants," said Annie. "I'll bet it leads up . . . to the Secret City."

"Yeah," said Jack. "Let's rest again . . . figure stuff out. . . . But first . . . check for snakes."

They both looked around carefully for snakes.

"All clear," said Annie.

She and Jack sank to the ground. They rested their backs against the first stone wall and took deep breaths. Jack felt sleepy and light-headed.

"Let's read about . . . Old Mountain," he said. He pulled out their travel guide and looked in the index. "Here." He read:

In the language of the Incas, *Machu Picchu* means *Old Mountain*.

"What? *Machu Picchu?*" said Jack, suddenly awake.

"That's where Uncle Josh went!" said Annie. "I saw his photos! He took a train up the mountain!"

"I know," said Jack. "Lots of tourists . . . go to Machu Picchu. It's one of the wonders of the world . . . like the Great Wall of China."

Jack turned the page. A photo showed crumbling stone ruins on a mountain ridge. The roofs of the buildings were gone.

He read:

The fortress of Machu Picchu was built almost six hundred years ago, at the height of the Inca Empire. It was a secret retreat for royal families and their guards and servants. Machu Picchu

**was active for only about a hundred years. After
the Inca Empire ended, the secret city fell into
ruin and was forgotten, until explorers discovered it in the early twentieth century.**

"Whoa," said Jack. "Topa and his grandparents are still calling Machu Picchu the Secret
City, so we've definitely come here hundreds of
years in the past."

"I know," said Annie. "Come on. We *have* to
keep going."

"Wait. We should rest longer. To get used to
the low oxygen," said Jack.

They took deep breaths and tried to relax.
Finally, Annie stood up. "I think I'm ready now,"
she said.

"Me too," said Jack. He felt a lot better. "Let's
give it a try."

He put away the travel guide, then turned

to Annie. She gave him a thumbs-up. Then she pointed toward the Secret City.

"I see a path," said Annie. She led the way to a pebble path that ran between the terraces up the slope.

"Not too fast!" said Jack.

They slowly hiked up the path. Clouds hid the higher terraces.

Through the haze, they saw people working in the narrow terrace fields. The workers were using wooden shovels to break up the hard ground.

Jack was glad the workers wore ponchos and hats like theirs. He was also glad it was hard to see through the cloud mist. Hopefully no one would notice two kids heading toward the Secret City.

"Keep going," Jack said. "Keep breathing."

They kept following the path. Near the top of the mountain, they came to the last terrace. A high wall loomed beyond it.

41

Jack was panting and covered with sweat. He and Annie pulled off their wool hats and gasped for air.

"I'm so thirsty," said Annie.

"Me too," Jack said. His throat felt dry and rough. "Keep going. . . ."

They climbed onto a large boulder and looked over the wall.

"Oh, man . . . ," breathed Jack.

All the mist had cleared away from the high mountain ridge. In the dazzling sunlight stood the fortress of Machu Picchu.

6

THE SECRET CITY

Rows and rows of buildings gleamed in the bright sunlight. The buildings were made of carved white stone. They had yellow thatched rooftops.

In the center of Machu Picchu was a grass-covered plaza. It was built on different levels. People were strolling up and down in colorful tunics and hats. Some wore red ponchos and long dresses. Most wore feathers and gold jewelry.

"We're the only people from *our* time ever to visit the living world of Machu Picchu," said Annie.

"Right," breathed Jack. "But don't forget this place is a secret. We're not supposed to be here."

"I know, I know," said Annie. "We have to find Cria fast. Do you see a baby llama anywhere?"

"No, they're probably not here yet," said Jack. "Topa said the way we came through the forest was faster than the Old Trail. Let's look at a map." He pulled out their travel guide and found a map of Machu Picchu.

"Here," he said.

Annie pointed to places labeled on the map. "Royal Palace . . . Temple of the Moon . . . Temple of the Condor . . ."

"Condor?" said Jack. "That's interesting."

"Right," said Annie. She looked back at the map. "Okay, here's the Sacred Plaza . . . and there's the Old Trail. That's the way the royal guards came with Cria. Should we try to get to the top of the trail and wait for them?"

"Yeah . . . no . . . I don't know . . . ," Jack said. "First I seriously need water."

"Me too," said Annie. "Look up *water*."

"I doubt it's in here," said Jack. But he turned to the back of the book and scanned the index. "Whoa! Listen to this: *Machu Picchu Water System*," he said. He turned to a page and read aloud:

Machu Picchu's water system was a famous feature of the city. The system collected rainwater, which flowed down a canal. Using the canal and rainwater, the Incas built sixteen fountains with clean drinking water available for everyone.

"Wow," said Annie. "Sixteen water fountains! We just need one."

Jack turned back to their book.

"Look," he said, pointing at the map. "There's one near the edge of the plaza."

"Great," said Annie. "Let's sneak over."

"No, don't sneak. We have to act like we belong here," said Jack.

"Right. Put your hat back on," said Annie.

They both put their hats back on. "I think we need more than just our hats," said Jack. He looked around and saw two wooden shovels propped against the stone wall. "Let's borrow those."

Jack and Annie each picked up a shovel.

"Whoa. This thing weighs a ton!" said Annie.

"No kidding," said Jack. "But we have to walk like it doesn't. Act like you carry it to the fields every day."

They swung their shovels over their shoulders.

"Let's go," said Annie.

Jack and Annie headed toward the fountain at the edge of the grassy plaza. They passed women in long red skirts holding babies. They passed kids throwing a ball the size of a basketball.

"Be cool," whispered Annie.

"Yep," said Jack, though he didn't feel at all cool. His shoulder felt like it was about to crack. His heart was pounding.

They passed a forge where workers were busy hammering metal. No one seemed to be paying attention to them.

When they reached the fountain, Jack was glad to see it was mostly surrounded by low stone walls. He and Annie slipped through a narrow opening. They dropped their shovels and pulled off their wool hats.

Sparkling clean water streamed from the mouth of the fountain.

"Whew!" said Annie.

She cupped her hands under the stream and drank. Then she stepped aside.

Jack took off his glasses. He splashed the cold water over his hot face and gulped as much as he could. He felt Annie shaking his shoulder.

"They're here! They're here!" she whispered.

"Who? What?" Jack said. He wiped his face with his poncho. He put on his glasses and peered through the narrow opening of the wall.

Two men were walking toward the plaza. They wore helmets with feathers and carried spears. They were followed by a line of white llamas roped together.

The parade of llamas made no sound, except for the tapping of their hooves on the stone pathway— and the ringing of a small bell.

"Hear that? A bell!" said Annie. "Look!"

She pointed to the end of the line. The smallest llama had silver fur and wore a collar with a bell.

"*Cria,*" whispered Annie.

7

NOW OR NEVER

"Are you sure that's Cria?" said Jack.

"Yes! She's the only silver one. She's wearing a bell. And she's tiny!" said Annie.

"Right, right," said Jack. "But we can't just charge over there and grab her. We need to make a plan."

"Make it fast!" said Annie. "She looks tired. She can't keep up with the big llamas!"

"I know. But look, they've stopped," said Jack. "Something's going on."

The two royal guards had stopped on the lowest level of the plaza.

Leaving the animals, the guards climbed up to the highest level. They entered a gate that led to the largest building on the plaza.

"The Royal Palace," said Jack, remembering their map.

A moment later, the two men returned. Four others followed them. They also carried spears and wore helmets with feathers.

"More guards," said Annie.

The men were guarding a tall man who walked behind them. The man wore a cape covered with glittering jewels. Gold earrings hung from his ears. His headdress was made of coils of gold with gold feathers that looked like rays of sunlight.

All the people in the plaza stopped what they were doing. Everyone stared at the glittering, golden man.

"Who is he?" whispered Jack.

"Check the book!" whispered Annie.

Jack pulled out their guide. He quickly found a painting that showed a man wearing the same clothes and headdress. He and Annie read together:

Emperor Pachacuti ruled the Inca Empire from 1438 to 1471. The fierce emperor was called Earth Shaker because he created the largest empire in South America. He also founded the secret city of Machu Picchu.

"I get it!" whispered Annie. "They took the baby llama as a gift for Earth Shaker. We have to get her back before they give her to him."

"Hold on, wait!" said Jack. "We need a plan!"

"No! Now's the time!" said Annie. "He and his guards aren't paying attention to her. It's now or never! That's the plan!"

Before Jack could stop her, Annie stepped out from their hiding place.

"Annie!" he whispered.

Annie started walking toward the llamas. Jack looked around. No one seemed to notice Annie. All eyes were on Emperor Pachacuti.

High on the plaza, the emperor and his men were talking. They, too, seemed unaware of Annie heading toward the llamas.

Annie walked casually to the little silver llama at the end of the line. She patted Cria's head and whispered in her ear. Then she tried to untie her. But she seemed to have trouble with the knot.

She's taking too long, Jack thought frantically. He had to help her.

Jack stepped out from his hiding place and headed toward Annie and Cria. He was terrified, but he tried to walk calmly.

Before he even got close, the baby llama broke free from the rope. She started sprinting across the plaza. She was heading away from Jack.

"Get her, Jack!" Annie cried.

People in the plaza laughed and pointed at Cria. Some Inca children started running after her.

Jack charged toward the baby llama, too. He reached her first. He grabbed her and wrapped his arms around her fuzzy silver fur.

Annie caught up to them. She held Cria's little head and looked into her eyes. "It's okay . . . ," Annie said breathlessly. "It's okay. We're taking you home to Topa."

The baby llama nuzzled Annie's hand. Before Annie and Jack could whisk her away, a man shouted, "Thieves!"

Jack turned and saw two royal guards hurrying toward them. Their spears were raised.

"We have to take her back home to her true owner!" Annie said boldly. "She belongs to our friend Topa!"

The guards reached for the llama.

"HALT!" someone shouted.

The royal guards backed off. Behind them, Emperor Pachacuti was striding toward Jack and Annie. Under his gold headdress, he had jet-black hair, dark eyes, and a rugged face.

"Who are you?" he said, glaring at them.

"I'm Annie, and he's my brother, Jack," Annie said. "And this baby llama is Cria. She belongs to our friend Topa. He is an orphan. He takes care of her like she is family."

Jack glanced at the guards. He didn't want to make them angrier. "She got lost on Young Mountain," he said.

"But these two nice guards must have found her," said Annie. She smiled at the men who had taken Cria. "We're happy to take her off their hands now and return her to Topa."

The emperor stared coldly at the baby llama. Cria stared back with bright, wide eyes. The llama's fearless gaze reminded Jack of Annie.

"I like this small animal. Her color is unusual,"

59

said the emperor. "I have none like her. She will stay."

Oh, no! thought Jack. *What now?*

"I'm sorry," said Annie. "But I'm afraid she doesn't want to stay here. She thinks it's pretty, and she thinks you're really great. But she wants to go home to the little boy who loves her."

"That's right," Jack said nervously. "That's—that's what she wants."

"How do you know what this animal wants?" the emperor said.

"Uh . . . well . . ." Jack didn't know what to say.

"I got this," Annie whispered to him. She looked at the emperor. "We know because she told me."

The emperor looked amused. "What? This llama talks to you?"

"Yes, she does," said Annie.

Oh, no, this won't work! thought Jack.

Annie looked at Jack. "She talks, right?"

Under her breath, she repeated their rhyme: *"Old legends will help you."*

Suddenly Jack remembered words from their guide: *Inca legend says that in early times, llamas could talk.*

"Um . . . yes, she talks to Annie," Jack said.

The royal guards laughed. The onlookers nearby murmured in low, excited voices.

"Show us," the emperor ordered. "Show us all how this little llama speaks."

8

ANCIENT MAGIC

Jack held his breath.

"No problem," said Annie. She knelt beside Cria and looked into her eyes.

The baby llama fluttered her long eyelashes.

"What do you want to do, Cria?" Annie asked her.

Then Annie put her ear close to Cria's mouth. She nodded as if the llama were whispering back to her.

Oh, no! He'll never fall for that, Jack thought.

Annie looked up at the emperor. "She says she would like to go home."

The emperor scowled. Then he broke into laughter. "I see, you are playing a children's game," he said. "You and your brother must leave now. I will keep the llama."

"Oh . . . wait, please," said Annie. "I'll tell her to talk louder."

"Annie—" said Jack.

"Shh," she said.

63

She whispered again in Cria's ear. Then she stared for a long moment into the huge eyes of the baby llama.

Cria stared back at Annie with an alert gaze. Then the baby llama began to speak.

"*TOPA*," Cria said in a tiny voice. "*GO BACK TO TOPA.*"

Jack couldn't believe it! He laughed out loud. How did Annie do that? How did Cria speak?

The emperor gasped and stared in amazement at the small silver llama. A hush came over the crowd. The guards and the people in the plaza watched with wonder.

"*TOPA,*" Cria said again. "*GO BACK TO TOPA.*"

"Hear that?" said Annie. "Topa is the boy who cares for her. She wants to go back to him. You heard her, right?" Annie turned back to Cria. "Say it again. Say it louder."

"*GO BACK TO TOPA NOW!*" Cria said clearly and loudly.

The emperor looked stunned. Then his face softened. "I understand she loves the boy," he said. "Her great feelings for him gave her the power of speech."

"Right," said Annie. "And Topa loves her, too. She is his whole world."

Emperor Pachacuti nodded. "You must take her back to him," he said.

"Really?" said Jack.

"Yes." The emperor looked around at his guards and the people watching. "The miracle llama has spoken. Her wishes must be honored."

"Thank you!" said Jack and Annie.

"Come, Cria. Let's go home to Topa," said Annie.

The baby llama took halting steps. The crowd silently parted to let Jack, Annie, and Cria pass.

Jack looked straight ahead. He didn't dare glance back. He was afraid the emperor might change his mind.

"Can't take her through the forest," Jack said quietly to Annie. "Go the way she came up, the Old Trail. It was marked on the map."

"Got it," Annie whispered.

"That way. Through the arch," said Jack. "Walk faster."

Jack and Annie walked faster. The silver llama took springy little steps beside them. She seemed to know she was going home.

Jack led the way to the stone arch. Guards stood on either side. They stared in awe at Cria as she pranced through.

On the other side of the arch, a rocky path led through the brush. Starting down the trail, Jack breathed more calmly.

"How did she do that?" he asked. "How did you make her talk? What happened?"

"I remembered our rhyme," said Annie, "and the words in the book about old legends that said llamas could speak. I believed it could be true. And Cria believed it, too. And she talked! Simple!"

"Not simple," said Jack with a grin. "Impossible!"

Annie, Jack, and Cria moved quickly down the winding trail. When they rounded a corner, Jack gasped and stopped.

They could see the long path ahead. The trail ran along the very edge of the mountain. Far below, the river raged between Old Mountain and Young Mountain.

"Oh, no," Jack said. "The trail looks just as dangerous as the bridge!"

"It's okay," Annie said. "We got this. Just remember, don't look down."

Jack forced himself to look away from the steep drop-off. "Okay," he said. "We have to go single file. Follow me, with Cria between us."

"No problem," said Annie. "Don't worry about us. Stay close to the side of the mountain."

Jack led the way as they started down the stone path. He could hear the soft click of Cria's hooves behind him, and the sound of her bell.

He forced himself to look straight ahead as he, Annie, and Cria carefully wound their way down the trail. A soft wind blew against the mountainside.

"Look, Jack!" said Annie.

"I can't. Don't ask me to look at anything," he said.

"But it's good news," said Annie. "I see the bridge. It's not far."

"Cool," said Jack. The bridge *was* good news—*and* bad news. How would they cross it with the llama? How had the guards done it?

"Oh, no, I don't believe it! Jack, look!" said Annie.

"I said I can't," said Jack.

"No, not down! Look up! Up at the sky!" said Annie.

Jack looked up. "Oh . . . whoa," he whispered. *Condors.*

9

SHADOW OF THE CONDOR

"You said condors prey on small animals!" said Annie.

"Sometimes maybe. Not always!" said Jack.

"What about now? Are they after Cria?" cried Annie.

"No, no. Stop. Stop walking," said Jack.

He, Annie, and Cria came to a halt.

Jack and Annie leaned against the mountainside. They looked up at the giant vultures circling overhead. One curved through the air and glided closer to them.

"We have to protect Cria!" cried Annie. She put her arms around the baby llama. "I'll carry her."

"No, you can't. She's too heavy!" said Jack.

"Then let's do it together," said Annie.

"No, the trail's not wide enough," said Jack.

"Then *what?*" said Annie.

"*I'll* carry her," said Jack. "I'm bigger than you."

Jack put his arms around the baby llama. He slowly and carefully picked her up.

"Ahh!" he said, almost falling over.

Jack got his balance. He took a deep breath. Then he began moving down the narrow trail with the baby llama in his arms.

"Hold her tight!" said Annie.

"I'm trying!" said Jack.

A condor floated closer. Its wide wings cast a shadow over them.

Jack couldn't believe how huge the bird was!

"Go away! Leave us alone!" Annie yelled.

"Cria's too heavy! We have to stop again!" said Jack. "We need another plan!" He lowered the llama to the ground.

Annie threw her arms around Cria, and Jack pulled out their travel guide. The baby llama let out high-pitched cries, as if she was terrified.

"It's okay, it's okay," Annie said, trying to soothe her.

"Hold on, be calm," said Jack. He found the page on condors. He read the caption under a photo:

The huge condors of the Andes once held a high place of honor. In old legends, they were portrayed as special creatures that carried messages from earth to the starry heavens.

"Oh . . . okay! I got this," said Jack. He closed the book. He knew what to do. He remembered another thing their guide book said about llamas:

The Incas once believed llamas were protected by a star constellation shaped like a mother and a baby llama.

"Hey there!" he called to the condor hovering above them. "Hey there, listen to me! Take a message to the starry heavens. Tell the llama constellation to look down on this baby llama and take care of her! GO! NOW! PLEASE!"

The condor floated for a moment. Then it dipped its wings and soared upward. The others followed. The flock of huge birds gracefully glided through the sky and disappeared behind the mountaintop.

"Jack, it worked!" cried Annie. "How did you do that?"

"I—I don't know. I did what you did with Cria for a moment. I believed the Incas' legends could be true," said Jack. "And I guess the condors believed that, too!"

"Great work!" said Annie. "To the bridge!"

Annie, Jack, and Cria started walking again

single file down the trail. Jack could see the rope bridge. The river far below roared and tumbled between mountains of rock.

When they reached the bridge, the baby llama tried to turn back.

"Wait!" said Jack, stopping her. He looked in her eyes. "Remember you crossed before? With the guards and the other llamas? You got this."

"You do," Annie said to Cria. "Plus, Jack and I are with you."

"I'll go first," said Jack. He stepped onto the swaying bridge. It rocked with every step he took. But he kept walking.

Jack heard Cria's bell ringing behind him. He heard Annie murmuring, "Good . . . good . . . you're doing great . . . keep going. . . ."

The sound of Annie's soft words and Cria's little bell gave Jack courage. Finally they reached the other side. One by one, they stepped onto the solid ground of Young Mountain.

"Safe!" said Annie.

"So far, so good!" said Jack.

Cria's bell jangled as she pranced around them.

"Take us to Topa!" said Annie.

"Follow me!" said the baby llama. And she took off into the cloud forest.

"Let's go!" Annie yelled, running after Cria.

"Wait, wait!" said Jack, charging after them. "Did I hear her say 'follow me'?"

"You heard it!" said Annie.

"Impossible!" said Jack, laughing.

Then he followed Cria and Annie through the ferns and over the roots and rocks, until he smelled woodsmoke and heard flute music.

In the clearing of the forest, Topa and his grand-parents were sitting outside their hut. The old man was playing a sad song. His wife was trying to get Topa to eat, but the boy waved the food away.

The baby llama bleated softly.

Topa lifted his head. "Cria!" he cried out, and the little silver llama ran to greet him.

10

The Secret of Brave

Cria's bell jingled as Topa threw his arms around her. "Thank you, Jack and Annie!" he said.

"How were you able to rescue her from the guards?" his grandfather asked.

"Um . . . we just found her," said Annie. "On the mountain."

"Yes, she must have escaped from the guards," said Jack. "And we brought her home to Topa."

"That is wonderful!" said Topa's grandmother.

"Catch me, Cria!" Topa said. The baby llama dashed after him across the grass.

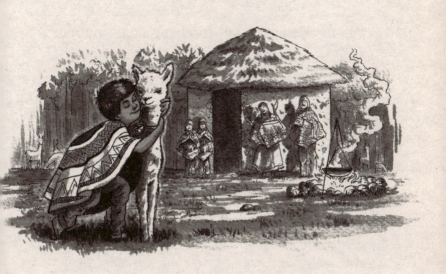

As Topa played with Cria in the meadow, his grandmother gave cups of water to Jack and Annie.

"Would you stay to eat with us?" she asked.

"Oh, I forgot! We still have our potatoes," said Jack. He took them out of his bag and handed one to Annie.

Jack and Annie ate their cold baked potatoes. Topa ate a potato, too. Then he pulled up some weeds for Cria. He fed the baby llama by hand, and she munched hungrily.

When everyone had finished their late lunch, they sat still for a moment. Cria and Topa were resting side by side in the grass. The old man started to play his flute again.

As the soothing music wafted through the air, Jack grew sleepy.

Annie nudged him. "Time to go home," she said.

"Oh, right." Jack stood up.

"Thank you for helping us," said Topa's grandmother.

"Good-bye, Jack and Annie! Thank you again!" Topa said.

"Take good care of Cria," said Jack.

"And, Cria, you take good care of Topa," said Annie, patting the baby llama's silver fur.

Cria fluttered her long eyelashes at Annie and Jack. She looked like she was smiling.

Jack and Annie waved and headed back into the cloud forest.

"Where's the tree house?" Annie asked.

"Follow me," said Jack. "I'm pretty sure I know where it is."

They pushed through tall ferns. They scrambled over rocks and roots. They wove around trees, until they came to the rope ladder.

"Yay! You found it!" said Annie.

She and Jack climbed up into the tree house. From a distance came the sound of the flute.

"That sweet music makes me miss home," said Annie.

"Me too," said Jack.

"Go back to Mom," said Annie, imitating Cria's tiny voice.

"Go back to Dad," said Jack.

Annie picked up their Pennsylvania book and found the picture of the Frog Creek woods.

"I wish we could go there," she said, pointing.

The wind started to blow.

The tree house started to spin.

It spun faster and faster.

Then everything was still.

Absolutely still.

A warm breeze blew into the tree house. The air smelled of summer leaves and sunshine.

Jack and Annie were wearing their shorts, T-shirts, and sneakers again. Jack's woven bag had become his backpack.

"Home," Annie said. "For the picnic!"

Jack reached into his backpack and pulled out *Travel Guide: The Andes Mountains of Peru*. He put the book on the floor. He took out Morgan's rhyme and looked at it.

"Uh-oh," he said.

"What?" said Annie.

"There's something in the rhyme we didn't do," said Jack.

"What?" said Annie.

"When did we find *the secret of brave*?" said Jack.

"Don't worry, we did that," said Annie. "Let's go." She began climbing down the ladder.

"Hold on," said Jack. He placed Morgan's rhyme on the floor of the tree house. Then he pulled on his backpack.

He followed Annie down the ladder, and they started through the Frog Creek woods.

"When did we find the secret of brave?" Jack asked again.

"Well, at first you were afraid to cross the rope bridge," said Annie.

"No, I wasn't," said Jack.

"Yes, you were," said Annie. "And you were afraid to enter the Secret City. And you were afraid to walk down the Old Trail."

"Okay, so what's your point?" Jack said, slightly hurt. "That I'm not brave? I already know that."

"No, that you *are* brave, *really* brave," said Annie. "You did those things even though you were afraid. I was afraid, too. But to us, saving Cria and bringing her home to Topa was more important than our fears. So we crossed the bridge. We entered the city. And we walked Cria down the mountain trail."

"So, we were brave after all?" said Jack.

"Yes. People can't be brave unless they're first afraid," said Annie. "Being afraid and being brave totally go together."

"Hmm," said Jack.

"That's the secret of brave," said Annie.

"Oh. Okay," said Jack. He took a deep breath.

"Hey, we'd better run. We're going on a picnic," said Annie. "Ready?"

"Ready for anything!" said Jack.

Then he and Annie took off running through the Frog Creek woods, heading for home.

85

Turn the page for a sneak peek at

Magic Tree House® Fact Tracker
Llamas and the Andes

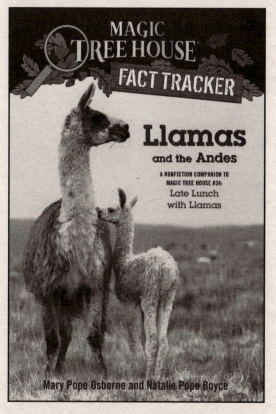

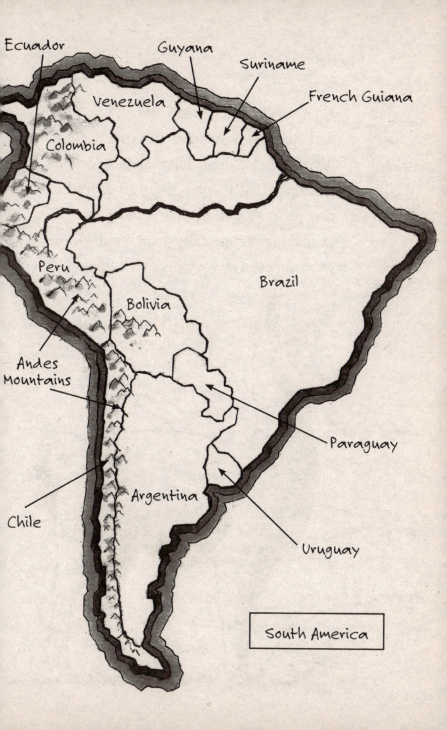

Ecuador

Guyana

Suriname

Venezuela

French Guiana

Colombia

Peru

Brazil

Bolivia

Andes
Mountains

Paraguay

Argentina

Chile

Uruguay

South America

Llama fat was made into candles.

Andeans dried llama and alpaca dung and burned it in fires for cooking and warmth. The dung also made excellent fertilizer that helped crops grow well in the poor mountain soil. Llama and alpaca dung is especially good fertilizer for growing corn at very high altitudes.

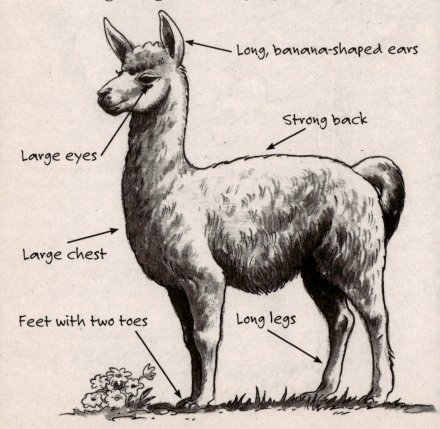

Long, banana-shaped ears

Strong back

Large eyes

Large chest

Feet with two toes

Long legs

How to Spot a Llama

Llamas can be over six feet tall and weigh about 400 pounds. Their long, banana-shaped ears stand straight up, and their hearing is excellent.

Many predators have eyes that focus straight ahead. Animals that are their prey, such as llamas, often have wide-set eyes. Large eyes on either side of their head give llamas a wide view of what's happening around them.

Llamas come in different colors. The most common are brown with yellow or white spots, but they can also be black, gray, and white.

Llama wool is tough and strong. It's great for making rugs, warm clothes, blankets, and ropes.

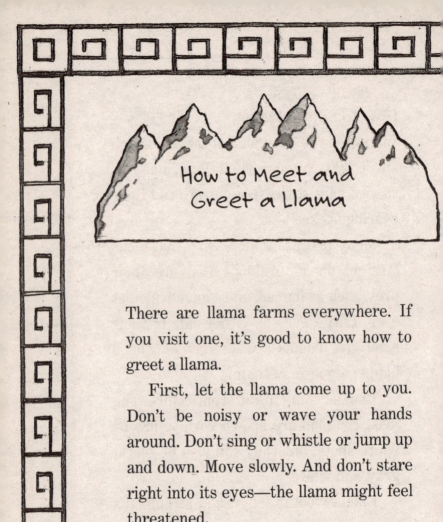

How to Meet and Greet a Llama

There are llama farms everywhere. If you visit one, it's good to know how to greet a llama.

First, let the llama come up to you. Don't be noisy or wave your hands around. Don't sing or whistle or jump up and down. Move slowly. And don't stare right into its eyes—the llama might feel threatened.

If the llama feels comfortable, it will sniff your face to get your scent. Otherwise, it will back away. Don't pat its head if it stays near you. Just try softly touching it on the sides of its neck.

Here's a special preview of

Magic Tree House® #35

CAMP TIME IN CALIFORNIA

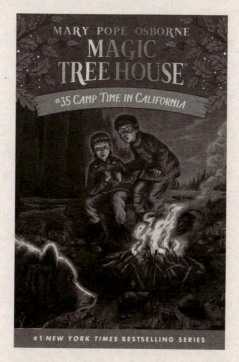

Visit Yosemite National Park

with Jack and Annie!

LAND OF GIANTS

Yosemite was cool and very dark.

"Mmm. Smells good," said Annie.

Jack inhaled the woodsy smell of damp earth, green leaves, and tree bark.

"It's too dark to see anything, but I can tell my clothes magically changed," said Annie.

Jack felt his clothes. "Mine too," he said. "Feels like I'm wearing a heavy jacket, long pants, and"—he reached down to his feet—"leather boots?"

"I think I'm wearing the same thing!" said Annie. "And my jacket has huge pockets. They're so big I can put my sketchbook and pencil inside."

"Great, me too," said Jack. He dropped his book and pencil into one of his jacket pockets. He put Morgan's message in the other.

"Where are we?" said Annie. "Can we see anything?"

Jack and Annie looked out the window. The branches above the tree house were dense with dark leaves. But between leaves and branches, Jack could see pale gray sky.

"Is it dawn?" asked Annie.

"Or dusk?" said Jack.

"Hard to tell," said Annie. "We'll find out soon. Let's go down."

"Okay, but go slow," said Jack.

"You too," said Annie. She found the opening in the floor and started down the rope ladder.

Jack followed. A mild wind blew through the

tree limbs. The leaves made swishing, whispery sounds.

"Hold on!" Jack called.

"You too!" Annie called back.

In the dark, Jack tightly gripped the sides of the ladder. He moved his hands and feet slowly down . . . and down . . . step by step . . . step by step. . . .

The breeze grew stronger, then softer. The *swishing* sounds rose and fell.

"This ladder's incredibly long!" Annie yelled.

"Yeah, because this tree's incredibly tall!" said Jack.

"Don't be worried!" said Annie.

"I'm not worried," said Jack. Actually, he *was* worried. *No tree in the world could be as tall as this,* he thought. The sound of windblown leaves was starting to sound spooky.

The high, sweet twitter of a bird came from nearby. Then another. And another.

It was dawn! "Yay," Jack whispered.

"It's getting lighter!" said Annie. "And we're almost there!"

Jack looked down. *Yes!* The ground was only about twenty feet below!

Jack and Annie kept climbing down. Finally they reached the bottom of the tree and stepped off the ladder.

"Hey, we *are* dressed alike," said Annie.

"Yep," said Jack. In the dim, shadowy light, he could see that their clothes *had* magically changed into canvas jackets, heavy cloth pants, and leather boots with laces.

Jack looked up. He could see a bit of pink sky above the treetop.

"Oh, man," he said. "This must be the tallest tree in the world! It's like a twenty-story building! And check out the trunk!"

"It's beautiful!" said Annie. She took off running around the massive reddish-brown trunk.

"I'll bet thirty kids could stand around this tree!" she said when she got back to Jack.

"More like fifty!" said Jack. "And all the trees look as big as this one!"

In the cool morning air, every tree seemed as high as a twenty-story building.

"Did we come to a land of giants?" Annie asked breathlessly. "Or did we shrink?"

Jack laughed. "Just the trees are giants," he said. "The squirrels are normal size, see?" He pointed to a squirrel scampering over the forest floor.

"Oh, right," said Annie. She looked around. "Is *this* the wilderness we're supposed to save?"

"I don't think so . . . ," said Jack. The gigantic trees looked super healthy and strong.

"Maybe there's another wilderness nearby?" said Annie.

"That doesn't sound right, either," said Jack.

"Well, we can figure it out later," said Annie. "I can't wait to start drawing." She pulled out her pencil and sketchbook.

"Seriously, I really can't draw," said Jack.

"Just try," said Annie. "I'll sketch that butterfly." She pointed to a delicate white butterfly perched on a leaf. "You can draw the squirrel."

The little squirrel was now nibbling a tree cone.

"Nah, too ordinary," said Jack.

"Do it for practice," said Annie. She crept closer to the white butterfly.

Jack opened his book. He set the sharp point of his pencil on a blank page and stared at the squirrel.

Suddenly Jack's pencil seemed to take on a life of its own. Before Jack could think, he drew the squirrel's head. He drew its dark eyes and small ears.

"Whoa!" said Jack.

"Wow!" yelled Annie, drawing the butterfly. "Our pencils are magic!"

"Yes!" cried Jack. He swiftly sketched the squirrel's body. He drew its long rear legs and short front legs and tiny hands holding the tree cone. He shaded the squirrel's fur on its belly, back, and bushy tail.

Soon he was done.

Jack smiled at the real squirrel. He knew the little creature really well now. It didn't seem ordinary at all.

"Look!" said Annie, holding up her sketch. "Perfect butterfly!"

"Perfect squirrel!" said Jack, showing his drawing.

"WE'RE ARTISTS!" cried Annie.

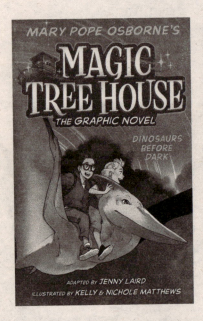